This Little Tiger book
belongs to:

_ _____

_____

For Harry, Katie (the real one), Lily and Ben, and for
my godchildren Isabelle and Archie. I love you all! - J H

To Isa - F S

LITTLE TIGER PRESS
1 The Coda Centre, 189 Munster Road, London SW6 6AW
www.littletiger.co.uk

First published in Great Britain 2015
This edition published 2015

Text copyright © Jenna Harrington 2015. Illustrations copyright © Finn Simpson 2015
Jenna Harrington and Finn Simpson have asserted their rights to be identified as the author
and illustrator of this work under the Copyright, Designs and Patents Act, 1988

A CIP catalogue record for this book is available from the British Library

Printed in China • LTP/1800/1149/0515

2 4 6 8 10 9 7 5 3 1

Katie McGinty Wants a Pet!

Jenna Harrington

Finn Simpson

LITTLE TIGER PRESS
London

Katie McGinty wanted a pet.

She wanted a pet more than ANYTHING in the world.

She wanted one more than Tommy Baker wanted to be a superhero.

More than Millie Phillips wanted to be able to stand on her head . . .

. . . and more than Hannah Hobbs
wished she had a sister.

But Daddy told Katie she had
to wait until she was a big girl.
So Katie waited, and measured herself every day . . .

4¾

4¼

4

2¾

1¼

until finally, she WAS big enough!

Katie was so excited she dragged Daddy off to the pet shop.
"Slow down, Katie," said Daddy, "and tell me
what kind of pet you want."

"Erm . . .
is it a hamster?"
asked Daddy.

"No!"

"How about a cat?"
he said.

"No!"

"I know!" Daddy cried. "You want a dog like Granny's."

No!

A chipmunk? A snake? A pig?

No! No! No!

"What I would like, more than anything in the world," laughed Katie, "is a . . ."

Daddy shook his head in disbelief. "Sorry, Katie, but you can't have a zebra as a pet. They live in Africa where it's hot. It's far too cold here."

"That's ok, Daddy," said Katie. "Granny can knit him a nice, warm, woolly jumper, and he can wear Mummy's ski boots on his feet."

"Hmm, but you just can't buy zebras in a pet shop," said Dad. "Besides, what would we feed him? We only have a small garden and there's not much grass for him to eat."

Katie shook her head.

"Don't be silly, Daddy!" she giggled. "He'll eat
pizza, and fish fingers, and spaghetti
with us at the table, of course!"

"And I suppose he
would have to sleep
in my shed?"
Daddy asked.

"Don't be silly, Daddy! He's going to sleep in my room in the bunk bed with me," Katie said happily. "In your bunk bed?" Daddy scratched his head.

BLACK BEAUTY

ANIMAL FARM

White Fang

THE JUNGLE BOOK

THE RED PONY

THE CALL OF THE WILD

"And will he have a bath with you too?" he asked.
Katie laughed. "Don't be silly, Daddy . . ."

". . . the bath is much too small.
I'll have to wash him at the swimming pool!"

"Katie, we are nearly at the pet shop," said Daddy. "I know you really want a zebra, but I'm afraid you just can't have one."

Don't worry, Daddy! I know I can't have ONE . . .

More magical books to share at bedtime!

DANGEROUS!
tim warnes

Mighty Mo
Alison BROWN

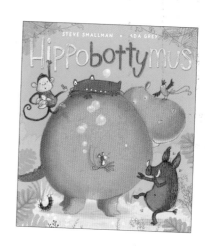

HIPPOBOTTYMUS
STEVE SMALLMAN • ADA GREY

BLACK BEAUTY

ANIMAL FARM
White Fang
THE JUNGLE BOOK
THE RED PONY

THE CALL OF THE WILD

THE FIRST SLODGE
JEANNE WILLIS • JENNI DESMOND

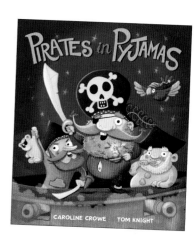

PIRATES in PYJAMAS
CAROLINE CROWE • TOM KNIGHT

POO IN THE ZOO
Steve Smallman • Ada Grey

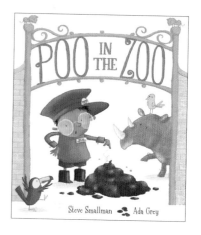

For information regarding any of the above titles or for our catalogue, please contact us:
Little Tiger Press, 1 The Coda Centre,
189 Munster Road, London SW6 6AW
Tel: 020 7385 6333 • Fax: 020 7385 7333
E-mail: contact@littletiger.co.uk • www.littletiger.co.uk